THE MYSTERY ON THE Oregon Trail

Managing Editor: Sherry Moss
Assistant Editor: Whitney Akin
Cover Design: Vicki DeJoy
Content Design: Randolyn Friedlander

Gallopade International is introducing SAT words that kids need to know in
each new book that we publish. The SAT words are bold in the story. Look
for this special logo beside each word in the glossary. Happy Learning!

Gallopade is proud to be a member and supporter of these educational organizations
and associations:

American Booksellers Association
American Library Association
International Reading Association
National Association for Gifted Children
The National School Supply and Equipment Association
The National Council for the Social Studies
Museum Store Association
Association of Partners for Public Lands
Association of Booksellers for Children
Association for the Study of African American Life and History
National Alliance of Black School Educators

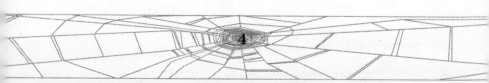

Christina   Mimi   Papa   Grant

Once upon a time...

Hmm, kids keep asking me to write a mystery book. What shall I do?

Mimi

Write one about spiders!

Papa said …

Why don't you set the stories in real locations?

That's a great idea! And if I do that, I might as well choose real kids as characters in the stories! But which kids would I pick?

MiMi, PiCK ME, PiCK ME!

ME, TOO, MiMi, PiCK ME, TOO!

Christina

Grant

Pick me!

You two really are characters, that's all I've got to say!

Yes you are! And, of course I choose you! But what should I write about?

National Parks!

 SCARY PLACES!

 Famous Places!

FUN PLACES!

Disney World!

New York City!

Dracula's Castle

GRAND CANYON

On the *Mystery Girl* airplane ...

I can FLY US anywhere!

Or aboard the *Mimi!*

Take me to the Forbidden City!

Or by surfboard, rickshaw, motorbike, camel ...

All great ideas! I can put a lot of history, MYSTERY, legend, lore, and laughs in the books! We can use other boys and girls in the books. It will be educational and fun!

Good stuff!

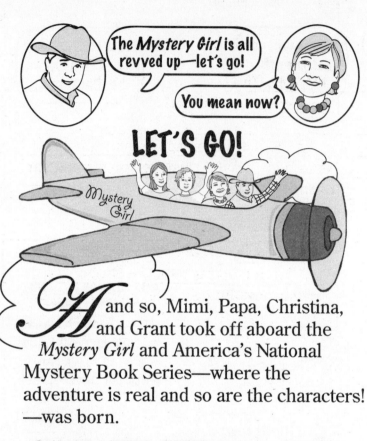

LET'S GO!

$\mathcal{A}$nd so, Mimi, Papa, Christina, and Grant took off aboard the *Mystery Girl* and America's National Mystery Book Series—where the adventure is real and so are the characters! —was born.

START YOUR ADVENTURE TODAY!

READ THE BOOK!

GO ONLINE!

TRACK YOUR ADVENTURES!

APPLY TO BE A CHARACTER!

Yikes! That was close!

Rats!

The Oregon Trail, Part I
by Christina

It's hard to imagine that Americans were once mostly clustered on a small part of the East Coast. It was almost like they got some "fever" that made many families want to pack up and head west to the wilderness, and hopefully a new and better life. Some families took the Oregon Trail to their new homes. They must have been very excited as they started out on this amazing journey. And now, Grant, and Mimi, and Papa and I are taking that same journey today. I think it will be fun?

1
GATEWAY TO THE WEST

Grant squished his face against the rectangular glass window and squinted. He shoved his messy blond hair away from his eyes.

"I think I can see Independence from here!" he said. He whirled around to have Mimi look and bumped right into Christina.

"OUCH!" Christina cried. "Um, that was my foot."

"Sorry, but I think I can see Independence from here," Grant insisted. "Look!"

Christina glared out the window, squinting her eyes against the sunlight.

"Nope, I don't think so. Independence is too far away," she said.

"But I know that's..." Grant argued.

"We'll be there soon enough," Mimi interrupted. "You two just enjoy the view. It's spectacular! They say you can see for 30 miles on a clear day like today!"

Grant and Christina couldn't argue with their grandmother because the view was amazing. They were standing 630 feet in the air at the top of the Gateway Arch in St. Louis, Missouri—the official start of the Oregon Trail. Grant felt like he was on top of the world!

"Did you know," Mimi began, "that the Gateway Arch is twice as tall as the Statue of Liberty and the tallest national monument in the United States?"

Grant shook his head silently, still mesmerized by the view. Christina watched the people below moving around like tiny floating toys. Her eyes scanned the flat western land she'd soon be traveling—not by car or bus or train—but by covered wagon!

"The view may be spectacular," said Papa in his booming voice, "but it sure is high up here."

"Come on, Papa," said Christina, "you're the cowboy pilot! You fly the *Mystery Girl* all over the world. You can't be afraid of heights!"

"Well, I'm in control of the Mystery Girl when I fly," Papa explained. "This arch is entirely different!"

Grant and Christina giggled at Papa's anxious expression. It was funny, and rare, to see him nervous in his big cowboy hat and tough leather boots. Grant and Christina knew their grandparents well and often traveled with them. Mimi was a children's mystery book writer, and Papa flew her anywhere she needed to go in his red-and-white plane, the *Mystery Girl*.

Suddenly, the tour guide chimed in on the intercom. "Thank you for visiting the Gateway Arch, America's Gateway to the West!"

That was their cue to make room for the next group of eager tourists. Grant and Christina gladly made their way to the tram that would take them on the steep return ride to the ground.

"Here we go again—the worst part of the whole trip," Papa grumbled. The ride to the top of the arch had not gone so well for Papa and Mimi. The family was crammed together in a little egg-shaped pod that zoomed up the inside of the arch. Mimi felt a bit faint and Papa's face was a bright shade of fire-truck red the entire time.

"What do you mean, Papa?" Grant asked. "The ride up to the top was the best part!" He grinned at Christina, who was also looking forward to the rollercoaster ride back down the arch.

"Yeah," Christina said, "maybe we'll get stuck!"

"Stuck?" Mimi asked, alarmed.

"Before we got here," Christina explained, "I read online that just a couple of years ago, the power went out in the tram. People were stuck in the thing for hours!"

"And that makes you excited?" Mimi asked, creasing her eyebrows in a frown.

"Oh, Mimi, it would be an adventure!" said Grant with a mischievous smile. "You love adventures!"

"Not that kind of adventure!" Mimi replied, almost shouting.

"No, sir-eee," Papa drawled. "An adventure like that is more of a BADventure!"

Grant and Christina giggled as their uneasy grandparents stepped into their tram car. Before the doors shut, Grant took one last look out the rectangular windows lining the inside of the arch.

"The Wild West! I can't wait!" he exclaimed. "Yee Haw!"

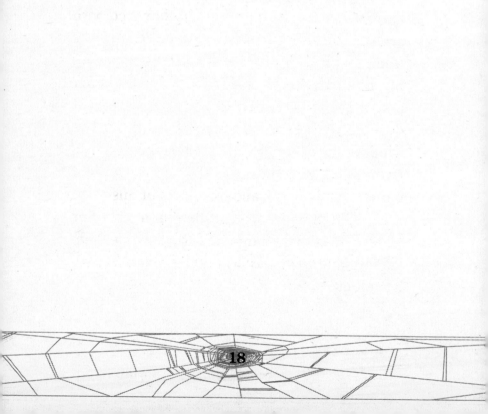

2

HOME ON THE RANGE

Christina slowly opened her eyes. Her long, shiny, brown hair stuck to her face with sweat. The sun blared down in the backseat of Mimi and Papa's rental car. Their drive from St. Louis to Independence, Missouri took longer than she expected and she must have dozed off. The last time she looked out the window, the scenery consisted of skyscrapers, rivers, and highways. Now, she saw nothing but flat land, grass, and dust—lots of dust!

Christina glanced at the seat next to her where Grant was busy clicking away on his video game. Christina nudged his side with her elbow.

"Hey, Grant, have you seen where we are?" she asked.

"Yeah, it's the prairie, duh!" Grant said, never taking his bright blue eyes off the video game screen. "You've been asleep forever!"

"It's a good thing you got some sleep, Christina," Papa said from the front seat. "We've got a lot of work ahead of us."

"Speaking of work," said Mimi, "there's the sign for Independence city limits right there!"

Christina watched the sign whoosh by and fade away as they sped down the highway.

"What is *that*?" Grant asked, pointing off to the side of the road at a long line of giant, white arches covering boxy, wooden wagons. In the front of each wagon were two horses attached with harnesses. They kicked at the dusty ground with their rough hooves and whinnied across the quiet prairie.

"That's a train of prairie schooners," said Mimi.

"Prairie whats?" Grant asked, confused.

"Schooners," Mimi replied. *"Prairie Schooner* was the nickname given to covered wagons..."

"I know why, Mimi!" Christina said, interrupting Mimi in the middle of her sentence.

"Alright, why?" Mimi asked, adjusting the sparkly red sunglasses perched on her nose.

"Because the white wagon tops look like sails from boats floating across the prairie," Christina explained.

"You're absolutely correct," Mimi said with a big smile. "Someone's done their research on the Oregon Trail!"

Christina glanced at Grant with raised eyebrows. He frowned.

"Well, I don't need to do research," Grant said, "I know how to be a real cowboy just like Papa. It comes natural!"

Papa nodded at Grant in the rear view mirror and grinned as he pulled the car to a stop. Grant and Christina jumped out of the car and raced toward the wagons.

"Whoa! Look at those wheels!" said Grant.

"Yeah, they're huge!" said Christina. "And these must be our clothes for the trip." Her expression changed as she held up two plain, scratchy, cotton dresses and two pairs of chocolate-brown work trousers with white shirts.

"Great, real stylish," Christina groaned and carried the larger dress to Mimi. She tried to imagine Mimi in a bland, cotton dress, much different from the trendy clothes and sparkly glasses she usually wore. Christina wondered if Mimi was cut out for life on the open range.

Mimi winked at her granddaughter. "This will be a new look for us," she said. "Isn't 'retro' the new fashion trend these days?"

Grant skipped back to the car to help Papa unload their supplies for the wagon. Papa pulled out blankets, a shovel, a barrel for water, a chest of extra clothes and shoes, and some pots, pans, and plates.

"Where's the TV?" said Grant.

Papa peered at Grant from beneath the brim of his jet-black cowboy hat.

"There's no electricity on the trail, Grant," he explained. "How would you watch TV?"

"I know, Papa," Grant said, smiling mischievously. "I was just joking. That's why I brought my video games with me."

"Video games, huh?" said a gruff voice from behind Grant. Grant slowly turned to see a tall, burly man with tanned, leather skin and a long, curly, gray beard. Grant's eyes grew wide. He looks like someone from a movie, he thought.

"This is supposed to be an authentic trail ride," the man said. "Video games, computers, cell phones, none of that's allowed!" The man looked very annoyed and Grant was about to apologize when another man came walking up. Well not exactly walking—he looked more like he was moseying on up to Papa's car in dusty, brown cowboy boots with shiny spurs, baggy jeans, and a long-sleeved, cotton shirt.

"Don't bother the kids, Chuck," the first man said, as the burly man walked away. "Sorry about him," he said to Grant. "He sounds mean, but don't let his curly beard fool you. He just runs the chuck wagon."

"The chuck what?" Grant asked.

"The chuck wagon that carries all the food," the man explained. "He'll make you three square meals a day out here on this trail so you best be as nice to him as you can. He gives the good ones mighty big helpings!"

"I'm Van, by the way, Wagon Master extraordinaire," the man continued. "Welcome to your home away from home. I'll be running this operation for the week, so keep up and listen up."

"Yessss SIR!" Grant said. He slapped the edge of his hand against his forehead in a salute.

"That's the spirit," said Van.

As the men walked away, Christina noticed the chuck-wagon man glaring at them from behind his horses. He grinned as his eyes met hers. Christina quickly looked away. Was that a nice grin or a sneer?

I don't think this is going to be the Oregon *Trail*, Christina thought. I feel scarily sure it's going to be Oregon TRIAL!

26

3

INDEPENDENCE MESS

One hour later, the car was unloaded and all their supplies were stacked on either side of the wagon.

"Let's get packin'," Mimi said with a tired look on her face.

"Wow," said Christina. "This wagon looked a lot bigger before we piled all our stuff next to it."

The four weary travelers stood staring at their supplies. The ten-foot-long and four-foot-wide wagon didn't look big enough for even half of their stuff!

"Well, the West is about adventure, new beginnings, and lots of hope!" Papa said. "So let's get started."

Christina climbed into the wagon and clattered around the wooden plank bottom. She rubbed the rough canvas cover on top. She thought about living in the small wagon for six months. The thought made her shudder. At least her trail ride would only last a few days!

"Christina! Are you in there?" Mimi called from around the corner. "We're just going to start tossing stuff in!"

Christina heard Papa say something like, "Wait! We have to organize..." but she was distracted. In the top corner of the wagon, she saw a white thread hanging from the folds of the canvas. She slowly reached for it and tugged. A piece of paper fluttered to the dusty floor.

"Hey whatcha doin' in here?" Grant asked, scrambling into the back of the wagon.

"Good grief! You scared me half to death!" Christina exclaimed.

"Sorry, but Mimi and Papa are arguing about how to pack the wagon, so I decided to come hang out with you." Grant said. "OK, but

keep it down, I've found something."
Christina said.

"What? A clue? Is it a clue?" Grant
asked, reaching for the piece of paper on the
ground. They seemed to always find clues on
their adventures.

"Hold on, I don't know," Christina said
as she picked up the folded piece of paper. "It
could be something left behind by the people
who used this wagon last."

"Well, what does it say?" Grant asked
impatiently.

Christina unfolded the paper slowly,
afraid it might be a mystery she wasn't
prepared for. The note was handwritten in a
messy scribble.

Be sure to pack only what you
need—flour, shovels, clothes,
and tea. Packing light is the
key to brave the dangers that
will be. No books, computers,
games, or TV. It's not
important what you read. Out
here it matters what you see.

"What do you think it means?" asked Grant.

"I don't know," Christina said. "It's probably just a friendly reminder from Van the Wagon Master."

"I don't think 'dangers that will be' sounds very friendly," Grant said with a worried look.

"Christina! Grant!" Mimi called from outside the wagon. "You two come out here for a minute. Papa and I have someone we'd like you to meet."

Christina quickly folded the mysterious note and gave Grant a "don't-you-dare-say-anything" glare. He nodded and they both jumped down from the wagon. They were in such a hurry that they didn't see the faded, splotchy-red fingerprints on the white canvas, right where the mysterious note had been stuffed.

4
HOME SWEET WAGON HOME

Outside the covered wagon, Papa and Mimi were standing with a boy and girl about Christina's age.

"Grant, Christina, meet Larry and Narci," Mimi said. "They're twins! They have come to the West for a great wagon adventure, just like us. Unfortunately, Larry and Narci's parents had to fly back home to take care of an unexpected batch of brand new puppies."

"We thought our dog was just fat!" Larry said. Grant giggled and held his belly until Mimi gave him "the look."

"And," Mimi went on, "their parents did not want them to miss out on all the fun, so we offered to let Larry and Narci tag along with our wagon. Would you two be alright with that?"

Christina looked at Narci. She was tall and thin with short blond hair and glasses. Her shirt sported a collage of brightly colored birds on it. Narci gave Christina a big smile and Christina grinned back. Maybe it wouldn't be so bad to have a friend on the trail.

"Of course! I could use another comedian on the trail!" Grant said, slapping Larry on the back. "You and me, we're going to be a team!"

"Christina?" Mimi said, looking expectantly into Christina's eyes.

"Sure, Mimi, I'd love to have Narci and Larry along," Christina replied.

"Great!" Narci said. Her eyes brightened and she gave Christina a hug.

"All right, you kids go get dressed while Mimi and I pack up this wacky wagon!" Papa said.

Christina grabbed her cotton dress and turned toward Narci.

"Nice to meet you," Christina said.

"You too!" Narci said. "You know you have the prettiest eyes, great for drawing, maybe I could draw you..."

Their voices faded as Christina, Grant, Narci, and Larry headed for the **outpost** to change into their western wear.

When the kids got back, Papa and Mimi were loading the last of the supplies onto the wagon. Papa gazed proudly at his organization. "Ah, a thing of beauty," he sighed, "a place for everything and everything in its place!"

"Don't you look spiffy!" Mimi said, tapping the top of Grant's black cowboy hat.

"Yeah, well, this cowboy stuff sure is itchy!" Grant scratched at his arm, his stomach, and his bottom.

"Yeah, and hot!" Larry added. He pulled his thick shirt away from his chest and blew a puff of air from his mouth. His forehead beaded with sweat.

"Well, you can't start complaining already!" Papa exclaimed. "We haven't even hit the trail yet!"

"Speaking of hitting the trail, are you pioneers ready to go?" said a loud voice from in front of the wagon. It was Van, clutching a giant map of the Oregon Trail. The map blew and crinkled in the hot, prairie wind.

"Our first stop is Fort Kearny," Van said, flattening the map out with his hands on the side of the wagon. He pointed to the spot with his chin. "If we get a move on, we'll be there by morning. So, let's head 'em up and move 'em out!" he shouted, as he made his way to the head wagon. Six other wagons lined up ahead of Grant and Christina's "prairie schooner."

Ahead of them, the massive wagon wheels slowly began to roll forward. The horses tugged against the harnesses and let out loud sighs as the drivers urged them along.

"Papa!" Christina cried suddenly. "Before we leave, I have to grab one thing out of the car!"

"Well, you better hurry, missy, or you'll be left behind. This wagon train is pulling out!" Papa said.

Christina raced to the car and grabbed a thin book stuffed under the driver's seat. Its cover featured a covered wagon and the words, "A History of the Oregon Trail" in fancy western letters.

Grant ran up behind her.

"Hey...come on...we're rolling out," he shouted, huffing and puffing.

"OK, I'm ready," Christina said.

"What's that?" Grant asked. "Didn't you listen to the clue? 'Pack only what you need.' I don't think you really need this book."

"You may not, but if I can't have my computer, I'm at least sneaking on a book. If we do have a mystery on our hands, I want to be prepared!" Christina grabbed the book and slammed the car door shut. The kids made it to the wagon just as Papa yelled, "Giddy up!" and slapped the reins on the horses.

I wonder what lies ahead, Christina thought. Adventure, or misadventure?

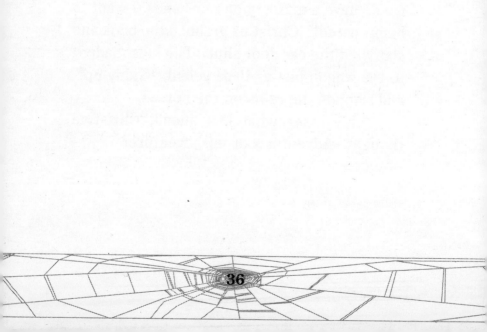

5

THE WHEELS ON THE WAGON GO ROUND AND ROUND

The wagon wheels slowly started rolling and they were off! Grant and Christina clutched the wooden slats on the side of the wagon. After a few minutes, Grant peeked through the canvas top at Papa seated on the front driver's bench.

"How fast will this baby go?" Grant asked.

"We're right at full speed now," Papa said.

Grant looked at the ground slowly passing by below. The grasshoppers were jumping faster than their wagon!

"I could walk faster than this!" Grant whined.

"Well, you're welcome to," Papa said. "Only be careful not to step in any horse poop! They tend to leave a pretty messy trail."

"Eww, Papa!" Grant said, crinkling his nose. "I think I'll take my chances inside the wagon."

"Suit yourself," Papa said with a grin.

The inside of the wagon was packed to the brim with trunks, suitcases, tents, and sleeping bags. There was barely enough room for anyone to sit. The wagon jolted along bumps and ruts, bouncing, bouncing, bouncing. Droves of dust poured through every nook and cranny. Grant soon noticed that being last in line on a wagon train was a bad idea—too much DUST!

After only a couple of hours, Grant wished he could slide back into their smooth-riding, spacious, air-conditioned, rental car. He needed some way to pass the time, so he looked at Larry, hoping for a distraction. Larry shrugged his shoulders.

CRRRRAAACKK!!!! Suddenly, the whole wagon began to wobble and shake.

Papa pulled back tightly on the reins and brought the horses to a quick halt.

"What was that?!" asked Christina, peeking out from a pile of clothes. One of their suitcases had tumbled down and clothing was scattered everywhere. It took Christina a minute to realize that Grant's underwear was hanging on her head.

"Ewww!" she yelled and quickly pulled the red-checkered boxers out of her hair. She threw them into a pile of clothes and shook her head and hands in disgust.

"Hey!" Grant said, offended. "They were clean!"

"C'mon you two, let's see what's going on," Narci interrupted, still giggling about the underwear.

Everyone jumped out of the back of the wagon. Papa stood next to the wagon with his head in his hands.

The driver's side wheel had broken. Half of the wheel was lying in the dust on the ground. The wagon was tilted to one side, creaking and groaning. It looked like it would topple over any second.

"Oh no, Papa!" said Christina. "What are we going to do?"

"Don't worry!" said a deep voice with a country accent. Christina recognized the voice as Wagon Master Van.

"Stuff like this happens all the time with these rickety old wagons," Van remarked. "There should be a spare wooden wheel stored on the bottom of your schooner. Lucky for us, we've got tools to help fix this thing. Way back when, a broken wagon wheel meant serious danger for the pioneers."

As the kids stood to the side and watched, Christina said, "I've got a bad feeling about this."

"What do you mean?" Grant asked.

"Remember the clue we found?" Christina asked. "It said, 'Packing light is the key to face the dangers that may be.' Van said that a broken wagon wheel could mean serious danger!"

"Yeah, but we've got tools to fix it," Grant said. "No danger here."

"I know," Christina said, annoyed that her little brother wasn't helping her with the clue. "But what if the broken wheel is just another clue in the mystery?"

"What are you trying to say?" Grant asked, slowly picking up on Christina's point. "Do you think someone set us up? Do you think the wagon wheel broke on purpose?"

"It's hard to say," Christina said with a serious look. "But it's definitely a possibility."

"Well, you know what we need to do," Grant said with determination. "Let's check out that wagon wheel. If it was a set-up, the wheel might have some clues."

"Clues?" said Narci. "Clues?" Christina said nervously. "Who said anything about clues? I didn't hear anyone say clues? Did you, Grant?" She hit Grant in the side with her elbow and glared at him.

"You mean you're not going to tell them?" Grant said.

"Tell us what?" asked Larry.

"Um, well, I...." Christina stuttered.

"Christina and I are trying to solve a mystery," Grant said. "We found..."

"I love mysteries!" Narci exclaimed. She smiled and stood tall. "My mom calls me

Sherlock because I can always figure out the mystery of a movie or book before the end."

"Yeah, and it's really annoying," Larry said, rolling his eyes.

"Good," Grant said. "You can help us figure out this one then. Let them read the clue, Christina."

Christina frowned at her brother and slowly handed the clue to Narci. Narci read each line slowly.

"So," Grant said expectantly. "What do you think?"

"I was just thinking that the wagon wheel accident is an eerie coincidence with this clue," said Narci.

"That's what we thought too!" Grant exclaimed. He glanced at Christina. "I told you it was smart to tell them the clue!"

"You did not," Christina argued.

"Well, I thought it," Grant said defensively.

"Yeah, and I guess you were right." Christina said, giving in. "It might help to have an extra pair of minds to help figure this out!"

Narci smiled widely at Christina.

"Good," said Grant. "Now let's go check out the broken wheel for clues."

The four friends walked through the tall grass around the wagon. They stopped next to the broken wheel that Papa and Van had tossed into the dirt. Larry picked up one of its carved spindles.

"These things are huge!" Larry said, standing the spindle up on the ground next to him. It was almost as tall as the top of his head.

"Hey, I think I found something," Grant yelled. Christina, Narci, and Larry quickly crowded around. Grant knelt by a piece of the wooden wheel. It was so big that all four of them couldn't lift it.

"I think I can read it from here," Christina said, rubbing her thumb along the shallow carvings on the inside of the wood. "It looks like a message!"

"What does it say?" Narci asked.

"It's hard to read, but I can make out some lines," said Christina. The clue said:

> *Your mail...may arrive faster than you will...Give it to someone named...*

Christina shrugged her shoulders. "I can't read the last word."

"Bill!" Grant exclaimed. "It says Bill."

"You're right, I see it," said Christina.

> *You might want to send home your will. This journey can weaken and...*

"Weaken and what?" Narci, Grant, and Larry yelled all at once.

"I don't know!" said Christina. "I can't read it."

"It's all smudged out," said Grant. He rubbed the edge of his sleeve along the smooth wood but couldn't make it out.

"Well, what rhymes with will and Bill?" asked Narci.

"Hill, mill, fill," Larry recited.

"Or KILL!" said Grant with a **terrified**, excited look on his face. "I think it's another clue!"

"I bet that's it!" said Narci. "But what does it mean?"

"Mail...bill..." Christina repeated. She rubbed her hand against her sweaty forehead in thought.

Just then, Papa came up, slapping the dust off his jeans. "Well the wagon's fixed, but it's about sunset so Van said we'll make camp here for the night." At the back of the wagon, Mimi was already setting up the tents and sleeping bags.

Christina tried to focus on enjoying her first night on the Oregon Trail, under the stars. But she couldn't help thinking about the two clues they had found. Was someone trying to ruin their trip? What could be so dangerous about the trail? Why would someone sabotage their wagon wheel? But more than anything, one worry kept her awake. Someone wanted her trip to fail, and they were close enough to hide clues in her wagon!

6
GREAT-GREAT-
GREAT-GREAT

After a hearty breakfast of fresh eggs, toast, and crisp bacon, Mimi and Papa loaded up the wagon. The train was on its way!

"I think I'm going to walk beside the wagon today," Narci told Christina. "I want to watch the prairie grass. I'm trying to sketch each day of our trip in my journal.

"Cool, I'll walk too!" Christina said.

"Me too," said Grant, raising his hand in the air.

"And me!" said Larry with an excited grin.

"Let's make sure it's OK with Papa," Christina suggested.

Before they could even ask, Papa gave them a nod and called, "Have fun, and watch out for those messy trails, Grant!"

"What was that all about?" Larry asked Grant.

"Don't even ask," Grant said. "Let's just say, be careful where you step."

Larry nodded and looked down. A stinky smell struck his nose. His boot was stuck in a tall pile of fresh horse poop!

"Messy trails," Larry said with a sigh. "I get it now."

Grant stared at Larry's foot and broke into giggles. "Well, at least you're not wearing flip-flops!" Larry scraped his boot through the tall prairie grass. Once it was clean, the boys ran to the front of the wagon train to hang out with Van.

Christina and Narci walked side-by-side for what seemed like hours over the flat prairie. The warm sunlight felt good on Christina's face. Narci was good company— quiet and cheerful. Every few minutes she would stop to sketch a bug or the movement of the grass in her little book.

"So, where did your name come from?" Christina asked. "I mean, it's pretty! But I've never heard the name Narci before."

"Yeah, it's a different name, but I'm proud of it," Narci said. "I'm named after my great-great-great-great-grandmother, Narcissa Whitman. She was one of the first women to travel on the Oregon Trial back in the 1800s."

"Wow!" said Christina. "That's so cool! Your grandmother's been on this trail?"

"Well, technically, she is my great-great-great-great *adopted* grandmother," Narci said. "She adopted my great-great-great-grandfather a long time ago. That's why my parents wanted to take me and Larry on this trip. The Oregon Trail is very special to our family."

"So what happened to your grandmother, I mean your great-great-great-great adopted grandmother?" asked Christina. "That's a mouthful! Did she make it to Oregon?"

"Yes!" said Narci. "She made it all the way over the Rocky Mountains. She and her husband built a house and became missionaries to the Indians. While she was living in Oregon, she adopted seven orphans whose parents died in a horrible accident on the trail. She raised them like her own children. My ancestor was one of those children."

"Wow," said Christina. "That's amazing!"

"That's why I'm so excited about this trip," said Narci. "I want to draw everything I see on the trail. By drawing, it's like I'm seeing everything the way she saw it long ago."

"Hey! Look at us!" Larry called across the field. Narci and Christina looked up to see the boys slapping the reins of Van's personal wagon! They were steering the horses left and right.

Christina and Narci laughed at their silly brothers.

But while she laughed, Christina had a creepy thought.

"Hey, Narci," she said. "What kind of accident did you say happened to your relatives on the Oregon Trail?"

"I didn't," Narci said. "My great-great-great-grandfather never found out what happened to his parents."

Christina felt a cold shiver in the heat of the prairie. What kind of danger lay ahead for her...and her family?

7
MAIL FOR SALE

"Look," said Narci. "Something's coming up ahead."

Christina shaded her eyes from the blazing sun. There stood Fort Kearny State Park rising tall out of the flat prairie.

"We're FINALLY here!" Christina said, excitement and exhaustion in her voice.

Van's wagon pulled to the back of the train. He had control of his reins again. Grant and Larry stuck their heads out the back of his wagon and waved.

"First stop—Fort Kearny!" Van called out across the wagon train. "Please take some time to look around. There's a nice post office and places to buy supplies inside."

Narci grabbed Christina's arm. "C'mon, I've got a letter I want to mail to my parents back home," she said.

"Wait!" shouted Larry, who had just jumped off Van's wagon. "I want to be there when you send it. It's from me, too!"

"Did you two have a fun ride?" Christina asked her little brother.

"Oh, it was wonderful," Grant said with a big smile. "You know, time seems to go by much faster when you're driving the wagon!"

The four young pioneers made their way across the sea of grass to the park. Narci found the post office in a group of buildings. She and Larry walked in to buy a stamp for their letter. Grant and Christina looked around for something to explore.

"Hey, Grant, that building says it has exhibits," Christina said. "Let's go there."

"OK," Grant replied, "as long as we don't stay too long. I want to check out the blacksmith shop. I heard clanging metal and I saw fire."

"Boys!" Christina said, rolling her blue eyes.

The two made their way into the exhibit hall. The soft lighting was punctuated by spotlights on selected pictures and artifacts.

"Man, this air conditioning feels so good!" Grant exclaimed. "I forgot what it felt like not to sweat!"

"The Pony Express!" Christina said, distracted.

"Excuse me? The Pony Express?" Grant asked. "Have you gone crazy, sister? There is nothing 'express' about the horses that are pulling our wagons."

"No," Christina said, pointing to the exhibit sign. "The *real* Pony Express."

"Oh, yeah," Grant said, scratching his head. "Um...what's the Pony Express?"

"Cool—the Pony Express!" said Larry, his voice echoing as he stepped into the dimly lit room with Narci.

"Did you mail your letter?" Christina asked.

"Yep, it should be there in a couple of days," Narci replied.

"It would have taken much longer on the Pony Express," said Larry.

"You know what that is?" Grant asked, impressed.

"Yes, I do," Larry said. "We just read about it in history class. But I didn't know Fort Kearny was its original home. This is cool!"

"The Pony Express was the name of a group of mailmen who carried letters on horseback across the West," Narci explained.

"You know about it, too?" Grant asked.

"Yes," Narci said with a smile. "Remember? Larry and I are twins and we're in the same grade."

"Oh...right," said Grant.

"They were the first postmen in the Wild West," Narci went on. "Except back then, it took 10 days to deliver the mail. They traveled on ponies all over the West from Missouri to California. They rode through prairie and mountains, and through wind, rain, and snow! And the most famous member of the Pony Express was Buffalo Bill!"

"Who was Buffalo Bill?" Grant asked.

"Probably the most famous cowboy of the Old West!" Larry replied. "He got his name because he was a buffalo hunter, hired by a company to supply buffalo meat to workers who were building the railroad."

"Yep," Narci added, "the Pony Express riders could travel up to 75 miles in one day! Lots of them were young teenagers who were light in weight and fast on a horse. It cost five dollars to send a letter on the Pony Express."

"Wow, that's expensive mail!" Grant said, digging his hands in the pockets of his itchy, brown pants and pulling out two quarters and a dime. "I could never afford to write home!"

"Guys," Christina interrupted. "That's it!"

"That's what?" Grant asked, confused.

"Our clue," Christina said, excited. "The Pony Express is our clue. *Mail...Bill...*our clue was about Fort Kearny and the Pony Express!"

"Yeah, that makes **sense**," said Narci. "The Pony Express sent mail and is known for Buffalo Bill!"

"But what does it mean?" asked Grant.

"I don't know," Larry said. "But it sounds to me like someone's trying to scare us off this trip."

The kids looked around the exhibit, suddenly afraid of the darkly-lit room. They all jumped when the big, glass doors behind them opened. Hot air swooshed in from the outside, reminding the kids of the long trail ahead. Mimi and Papa walked in. Mimi was waving a white envelope in her hand.

"Grant! Christina!" she called. "You've got a letter!"

"A letter!" Grant said. "Cool!"

"From who?" Christina asked, suspicious.

"I don't know; it doesn't say," Mimi answered. "Why don't you open it?"

Christina took the letter from Mimi. The outside handwriting was addressed to them at Fort Kearny. Who would know where they were? Christina slowly tore the edge of the envelope and lifted out a folded piece of paper. As she unfolded it, she recognized the messy handwriting!

"What is it?" Mimi asked, curious.

"Oh," Christina said quickly, stuffing the note back in the envelope. "Just a letter from a friend who knew we were on the Oregon Trail."

"Well, that's awfully nice," Mimi said.

"Meet us at the wagon in five minutes," boomed Papa. "This train's a leavin'!'"

Papa and Mimi sauntered out the doors again, arm in arm, leaving the kids alone.

"What friend?" Grant asked Christina.

"Well, not exactly a friend," Christina said. She pulled the letter out of the envelope and unfolded it. Narci gasped at the sight of the handwriting.

"Another clue!" she said. "What does it say?"

Your wagon wheels are not the first. Many trails have marked this dirt. Some have traveled calmly forth, but others followed with a curse.

Christina looked up at Narci, Grant, and Larry. They all looked terrified.

"Are we the ones that go 'calmly forth'?" Grant asked, his voice squeaky. "Or are we the ones with the curse?"

"I don't know!" Christina said.

Just then, a loud announcement boomed through the building's intercom.

"The wagon train is moving out!" It was Van's voice.

"We better go," Larry said.

The four made their way from the exhibit, but Grant lagged behind. What if their wagon was cursed?! He couldn't get the thought out of his mind.

8
SEARCH FOR A CURSE

After another night of camping, Christina was longing for her comfortable bed. Sleeping under the stars might be fun, but sleeping on top of rough, flat ground was not! At least she could smell the hot bacon sizzling over the campfire.

Christina made her way down to the chuck wagon. She learned that it originally got its name because it was just an actual kitchen nailed onto the back of a wagon. She grabbed a tin plate of bacon and sourdough biscuits.

Everyone was up and moving by the time she returned. Mimi had packed the tents and sleeping bags, and Larry and Narci were loaded up in the wagon ready to go.

"Where's Grant?" Christina asked.

"I don't know," Mimi said. "Last time I saw him, he was looking at the wagon wheels. I have no idea why."

Christina walked to the side of the wagon and found Grant hunched over in the tall grass outside of the wagon circle.

"Grant! Are you ok?" Christina asked, running to him.

Grant stood up. He held a long piece of prairie grass. "I'm just checking out our surroundings."

"Oh, good, I thought you were sick or something," Christina said. "What exactly are you looking for?"

"Oh, nothing in particular," Grant said. "Just anything that looks curse-like or creepy."

"What?" Christina asked, surprised by Grant's answer.

"The clue said that some wagons were cursed," Grant said. "I just wanted to check ours out and make sure we weren't one of *those* wagons."

"You mean you're looking for a physical curse?" Christina asked, eyeing her brother.

"I don't think you can see and touch curses. They're just a curse."

"Well, better safe than sorry," Grant said. "And so far, I've found nothing out of the ordinary."

"Right," Christina answered. "Except for a creepy clue in the wagon canvas, a broken wagon wheel with a carved inscription, and a mysterious letter at Fort Kearny. Yep, that's nothing out of the ordinary."

"Oh man," Grant whined. "We *are* cursed!"

"No we're not, Grant," Christina said. "We're fine, you'll see."

They got back to the wagon just as the train was pulling out. Van yelled back at the wagon train, "NEXT STOP, ASH HOLLOW! GIDDY UP!"

9
STUCK IN A RUT

The trains came to a rough halt in Ash Hollow. The ride was bumpy, as usual, but the thoughts of a looming mystery kept the kids occupied. When they peeked out of their wagon, they saw a beautiful landscape of bright green grass and small rolling hills.

"Welcome to Ash Hollow," said Papa. He helped the kids jump out of the wagon one by one. "Van says this place is mostly known for its walking trails. I think you might find something pretty neat up that one."

Papa pointed off toward the left where a small footpath led up a hill to level ground.

"Let's go see!" Grant said, excited to follow Papa's suggestion.

Grant and Larry scrambled up the hill ahead of the girls. They stopped when they got to the top and stared.

"What is it, guys?" Christina asked. "Is something wrong?"

"Whoa, Narci, you've got to see this," Larry said.

Christina and Narci climbed up the path as quickly as they could. At the top, they stopped and stood by the boys in amazement. On the ground in front of them were two large ruts cut into a piece of grey rock.

"Wagon ruts," Christina said, her voice filled with wonder. "These are the ruts created by the original wagons. So many people drove over this very spot that their wheels formed these." She spread out her hands pointing to the long line of ruts cut in the rock.

"Wow!" said Grant.

"I've got to draw this!" Narci said. She pulled out her sketchbook and scribbled away. "Do you think my grandmother traveled this path?"

"You mean your great-great-great-great adopted grandmother," Larry said, correcting his sister.

"Huh?" Grant asked, very confused.

"I bet she did, Narci!" Christina said, excited by the thought. "It's like a little piece of her is right here."

"Speaking of pieces," Grant said. "I think I just put some pieces together."

"Grant," Christina said, annoyed. "What are you talking about?"

"Pieces of the clue!" Grant exclaimed. "Remember, it said our wheels were not the first, many trails have marked this dirt. Well, there are the marks for ya!"

"You're right, Grant" Christina said, surprised that her little brother figured it out.

"I think I might know what the second part of the clue means," Larry said thoughtfully. "It said some wagons made it through smoothly—like grandma Narcissa's wagon. But some were cursed—like great-great-great-grandpa's wagon. They never made it through."

"I think you're onto something," Narci said. "This must be where the clue was leading us. Let's look around and see if there's another clue here."

The kids walked beside the ruts looking for clues. Grant jumped down into one rut and walked along where the wagon wheels had passed. The cuts in the rock were so deep the top of the ground was even with his waist!

"Look up there," Christina shouted. She pointed up the path to something shining in the sun.

Larry ran to the object first. He picked it up and turned it around in his hands.

"What is it?" Christina asked, out of breath from running.

"I think it's an old horse shoe," Larry said holding the U-shaped metal object in the air.

"Wait, look, there," Narci pointed. "There's something taped to the side of it."

Larry pulled off a thick piece of grey tape and a piece of paper unfolded.

"What does it say?" Grant asked.

Larry flattened out the piece of paper.

"Well that's not surprising," Christina said. "It's in the same scribbled handwriting as the last clues. Whoever's doing this is a one-man team."

Don't get stuck in a rut, this path leads to jail.

"What?" Grant said. He looked up with concern. "I haven't done anything, I promise. Well, I mean, once I tried to drive Papa's car, but it didn't work. I was just pretending..."

"Grant, calm down," Christina said. "The police aren't after you. You're in the middle of nowhere in Nebraska! It's a clue. Someone's trying to tell us something."

"Do you think they sent pioneers to jail on the Oregon Trail?" Narci asked.

"I don't know." Christina said. "But we've got to figure this out."

"Let's talk about it over dinner tonight," said Larry. "I need some time to think."

The four made their way back down the trail. They were too busy watching their step to notice Papa watching them from a distance. On his face was a big, amused smile.

10

COWA DUNGA

That evening, Van corralled the seven wagons on the train into a big circle. The setting sun cast a red-orange glow on the prairie scene.

"Hey Larry!" Grant said, interrupting the peaceful quiet. He was carrying a big bucket with both hands. "Van wants us to go get some fuel for the fire. The boys hurried over to Van's wagon for instructions.

"As you can see," Van said. "There aren't many trees out here on the prairie. Lots of grass, that's for sure. But we found out long ago that grass doesn't burn well."

"So, what are we going to use for the fire?" Grant asked curiously.

"Well, that's where you come in," Van answered. "The best burning stuff around is bison chips."

"Bison chips?" Larry said. "What are they?"

"Well, city boys, they're dark and round and hard. You know, bison chips," Van said, grinning. "Most of the bison got killed off when the pioneers began settling the West. They killed the bison for their meat and left the carcasses to rot."

"Gross!" said Larry.

"So now we use cow chips," Van explained.

"What do you mean?" Grant asked. "Like cow potato chips?"

"Like cow dung!" Van said.

"By dung, you mean poop, right?" Larry asked.

"Well, yes, technically," Van said. "But cow chips are dried so they're not squishy or smelly. Just think of them as pieces of firewood."

"So, where are we supposed to find these cow chips?" Larry asked.

"Out there," Van said, pointing to the open prairie. "Cattle herds pass through here all the time. They do their business. The sun dries it up. And *voila*—cow chips!"

"And why do we have to do this job?" Grant asked.

"On the trail, everyone has to pitch in," Van said. "Plus, I've done it before, and it's disgusting, so good luck!" He quickly walked away.

"Ooookkkkaaay," the boys said together, dreading their chore.

In half an hour, Grant and Larry were back with a bucketful of cow chips. They walked right up to the middle of the wagon circle and presented their find to Van, who was clearing the ground for the fire.

"Well I'll be, boys!" Van said. "You've gathered enough cow chips for the rest of the week. Where did you find all of these?"

"Let's just say, our feet led us in the right direction," Grant said. He lifted up his boot for Van to see the smelly remains of walking through a cow field.

"A job well done!" Van said, holding his nose with his fingers. He patted Grant on the head and tossed some chips into the fire. "Chuck, we're ready to start dinner when you are," he yelled.

Chuck stomped out from behind his wagon carrying a sack of rice—and bacon, of course. A hearty meal of boiled rice, crispy bacon, and hot tea was ready in no time. The kids stood in line at the fire and received their food on blue and white speckled plates. They ate quickly with a "yum" and "mmmhmm" mumbled in-between bites. The long ride had worked up quite an appetite!

After dinner, the families from all seven wagons gathered in a circle around the fire.

"This is when the original pioneers would sing, dance, act out skits, or read," Van explained to everyone. "Usually I try to sing a country tune of my own, but lucky for y'all, we have a special treat tonight. I think you'll find this much more entertaining than my nightly song—I have been known to make the coyotes howl."

The crowd laughed at Van's joke then hushed as the "special treat" entertainer stepped to the center. Grant and Christina were shocked when they recognized the special entertainer was Larry! In his hand was a beautiful hand-carved wooden fiddle.

"Hey, you didn't tell me you played the fiddle!" Grant said across the fire.

"You didn't ask!" Larry said. "I've played the fiddle since I was five and I learned some campfire songs just for this trip!"

Larry pulled the bow quickly across the tight strings of the fiddle and began a lively tune of "Old Susannah." Everyone around the fire clapped and sang along. Some couples even got up and did a cowboy line dance.

The last song Larry played was a peaceful lullaby to end the night. When the music stopped, Grant was asleep with his head rested on Christina's shoulder. She wiggled her shoulder. "Huh, what? Is it morning already?" Grant said, confused and tired.

"No, silly, it's bedtime, said Christina. "Let's go back to our tent. We've got a long day ahead of us."

Grant slowly walked to his tent, rubbing his groggy eyes. He needed to get his sleep. Tomorrow might be his first night in jail!

11

JAILHOUSE ROCK

Christina stared at the prairie ahead of her. It was so flat! The swaying grass looked more like an ocean than a field.

"Mimi?" she asked, trying to break the silence of the wagon ride. Bumping along the trail was getting pretty old. "Where are we stopping next? I don't see anything for miles."

"You'll know when we get there," Mimi answered. "You can't miss it."

Christina sighed and stared at the ground again. She was almost thankful for the mystery, even if the clues were scary. This endless prairie with nothing to do was about to make her crazy! She decided to focus on the last clue. She was almost positive that the clue

wasn't talking about an actual jail. Her Oregon
Trail book never said anything about Oregon
jails! But what did it mean?

"Hey, look!" Grant shouted from the
driver's seat where he was sitting with Papa.
"I think I see something up ahead!"

Christina poked her head out of the
opening at the front of the wagon. She
squinted and looked far into the distance.

"I don't see anything," she said.

"Over there!" Grant cried, pointing
toward his left. "Look up."

Christina followed Grant's finger. Sure
enough, in the distance, she could see a shape.
It looked like it was rising out of the prairie
straight up to the sky.

"I see it!" Christina shouted.

"I told you that you wouldn't miss it,"
Mimi said. "It's pretty amazing. The pioneers
called it Courthouse Rock and right behind it
is Jail Rock."

"Oooohhhhh," Christina said. The clue
made sense now. Not a jail, a rock!

"What's so interesting?" Mimi asked.

"Nothing!" Christina said quickly. "Um, I was just looking at how amazing it is. We haven't seen anything for miles and there it is." Christina couldn't take her eyes off the two buttes, hundreds of feet high, jutting up out of the prairie. She wondered what the first pioneers who crossed the trail thought of the giant "jail."

"Mimi," Grant asked, his eyes still glued to the giant, rock structures, "what state are in we now?"

"We're in Nebraska," Mimi replied, "just about right in the middle of the United States of America!"

When they were close to the base of the rocks, the wagon train slowed to a stop. Grant and Christina started to climb out of the back of the wagon on their way to search for more clues.

"Whoa there!" Van said, standing tall, hands on hips. Grant almost kicked him in mid-jump. "What's your hurry?"

"We're going to explore the rocks!" Grant said impatiently.

"Sorry, buckaroo!" Van replied. "We won't have time for much exploring today. We're on our way to Scotts Bluff. I want to make it there before nightfall. We're just stopping here at Jail Rock for some quick grub.

"In fact," he continued, "I heard Chuck saying he could use some help getting lunch together. Why don't you four kids go get the plates ready?"

Grant and Christina looked at each other. Chuck. As in chuck wagon Chuck! They slowly walked away from Van and found Narci and Larry.

"I'm not going in that chuck wagon, and I'm certainly not going near Chuck!" Grant said.

"He's not that bad," Larry said.

"Come on, Grant, we have to," Narci said. "We're together; we'll keep each other safe. What's he going to do in broad daylight anyway—turn you into chuck-wagon stew?"

Grant sighed and followed his three friends. At the chuck wagon, Chuck had started a small fire with cow chips. Larry bravely walked up to Chuck.

"Hi," Larry said, trying to sound **confident**. "Van told us you could use some help getting lunch ready."

"Uh, yeah, sure," Chuck grumbled in a low, annoyed voice. "Plates are in there." He pointed to his chuck wagon.

"Oh," Larry said. He motioned for the other kids to follow. The wagon was filled to the top with sacks of rice, flour, tea, coffee, and LOTS of bacon. One side of the wagon was lined with stacks of blue and white speckled plates and tin cups.

"I guess we should just start grabbing plates," Narci said.

They each took a deep breath, stepped into the wagon, and got to work. Narci pulled plates off the big pile in the corner. She handed them back in an assembly line to Grant who set the plates outside on a table.

"This isn't so bad," Christina said. "I don't see any scary looking things. It just looks like a kitchen pantry."

"Uh, Narci?" Larry said. "How about passing some more plates back?" Larry was waiting behind Narci empty-handed. The assembly line came to a halt. Narci stood perfectly still.

"Guys, I think I found something!" she said.

She passed back a folded piece of paper to Christina.

"Oh, my gosh!" Grant said. "Another clue! I knew something was up with Chuck!"

"Chuck wouldn't plant a clue in his own wagon," Christina said.

"What does it say?" Larry said. "Read it out loud!"

> Beware of this cliff, it's hard to escape, use caution and skill or you'll meet your fate, like Hiram did in that fated place.

"Great!" Grant said. "Another creepy clue about death and fate and disaster."

"What's taking you guys so long?" Chuck's gruff voice startled the kids.

"We'd better get out of here before Chuck finds out about the clue," Larry said.

They jumped out of the wagon and handed Chuck the last plate. Christina stuffed the new clue in the pocket of her cotton dress and bit her lip. What did this new warning mean?

84

12
A BIG THUMBS UP!

Back in the wagon after a quick lunch of beans and biscuits, the kids quietly discussed the new clue.

"Who do you think Hiram is?" Narci asked.

"I don't know," said Christina. "I'm trying to find something about him in this book but I can't find anything."

"I'm more worried about how the clue made its way into Chuck's wagon," Larry added. "I guess that rules him out as a suspect. Who would hide a creepy clue for us in their own wagon?"

"Yeah," Grant said. "And how did they know we'd be in Chuck's wagon anyway?"

"Van!" Christina shouted. "Do you think it could have been Van? He suggested we help Chuck and Papa said he told us we'd find something interesting on the trail at Ash Hollow."

"Van?" Narci said, skeptically. "Van's so nice and he's always around. I don't think he'd do that."

"But he is the wagon master," Larry said. "He knows exactly where we'll be going next."

"I don't know," Narci said. "I just don't think Van's our mystery man."

"Well, regardless of who it is," Christina said, "we've got a clue to figure out!"

"Look to your right!" Mimi yelled back into the wagon. "You'll want to see this!"

The kids stuck their heads out all at once. In the midst of the prairie was another giant rock pointing straight up to the sky like a rocket.

"Wow," Christina said, "that one's even taller than the last one!"

"I've got to draw this," Narci said. She whipped out her sketchbook while Christina thumbed through her Oregon Trail book.

"Here it is," she said. "Chimney Rock! It was one of the most popular landmarks for the pioneers." She read on. "Listen to this, Narci! 'Pioneers often drew pictures of Chimney Rock to remember the spectacular landmark. Today, hundreds of drawings of the rock are preserved as historical artifacts.'"

"That's amazing," Narci said. "I feel like a real pioneer."

"It doesn't look like a chimney to me," Larry remarked.

"Yeah," Grant agreed, "it reminds me of a big 'thumbs up' rising out of the prairie. Do you think it's a good sign? Maybe the rock's a clue that what's ahead isn't so bad?"

Narci looked down at her drawing book. Her sketch did look a little like a "thumbs up." Maybe Grant was right...

13
CALL YOUR BLUFF

"I think this has been the longest travel day yet," Grant complained. "It seems like we've been on this trail for weeks!"

"Don't worry," Mimi said. "Scotts Bluff is just ahead. We'll make camp there for the night. Tomorrow's a new day. And I think you'll like where we're going."

The wagons circled around Scotts Bluff and stopped in their traditional corral. The bluff looked like a steep cliff with rocks around the edges. It loomed in the distance as Christina and Narci set up camp for the night.

"What does your book say about Scotts Bluff?" Narci asked Christina.

"One of the pioneers described it as looking like a huge fortress," Christina remarked. "The wagon trains used it as a landmark for navigation. It's where the Great Plains leave off and the foothills of the Rocky Mountains begin.

"I found something about Hiram in my book, too," Christina added, as Narci unfolded her sleeping bag. "It said that Hiram Scott was a pioneer who traveled over the bluff. He had a terrible accident and died. They named the bluff in honor of him."

"Oh, how sad!" Narci said. "What do you think it has to do with our clue?"

"I don't know," Christina said. "We need to check out the bluff more closely and search for more clues."

"I'll get the boys!" Narci said.

Mimi and Papa were distracted helping Chuck with kitchen duty and didn't see the kids slip away through the tall grass toward the bluff. They got there just as Van rang the bell on the chuck wagon, signaling dinnertime.

Grant's stomach growled. "Aww man, are we going to miss dinner?" he asked.

"We've got more important things to think about right now," Christina said. "Help me look for some sort of clue."

"Look!" Narci said. "More ruts."

"Yeah, there are ruts all over this rock," Larry pointed out.

"The wagons must have traveled over the bluff instead of around it," said Christina. "There's got to be a clue around here somewhere."

"This is more like a cliff than a rock!" Grant said. He gazed up at the tall, steep, rock wall. "Do you think I could climb to the top?"

"Don't even think about it!" Christina said. "You'd break your neck."

For the rest of the evening, the kids wandered around the base of the rock, searching for clues. They found nothing.

"Guys, I'm starving!" Grant announced. "I don't think there's anything here."

"There has to be!" Christina insisted.

"Sorry, Christina, but I think Grant's right." Narci patted Christina's shoulder. "We should probably head back."

"Um, it's getting dark, fast," Larry said. He pointed to the sky. None of them had thought to watch for the sunset. Now the big, orange ball was fading fast into the distance. Stars were prickling the periwinkle sky.

"What are we going to do?" Christina asked. "We can't walk back in the dark. There are snakes, cougars, and who knows what else!"

"We can't stay here either," Narci said, just as worried as Christina. "What if we don't make it back to the wagon train before it leaves?"

"What if we don't eat dinner??!!" Grant said frantically.

"I could probably find some bugs or something for you..." But before Larry could finish his sentence, they heard a rustle in the grass.

"Did you guys hear that?" Christina whispered.

"Yeah," said Narci. "And it didn't sound good."

The four kids huddled together. *SSHHHH. SSHHHH.* Christina was ready to scream! The grass rustled one last time and out popped Chuck!

Narci let out a soft cry and Christina held her breath. Chuck's shadow looked like a giant against the backdrop of the bluff. He reached out his hand to Grant.

Grant stayed perfectly still except for shivers running down his spine.

"Take my hand, kid," Chuck said. He pulled out a lantern. "Follow me back."

Slowly, the kids rose and followed Chuck through the tall prairie grass. He led them straight to the wagon where Mimi and Papa were waiting nervously.

"Where were you?!" Mimi cried, hugging Grant and Christina at the same time. "I thought something terrible had happened."

"We just wanted to explore the bluff, but we lost track of time," Christina explained.

"Sorry, Mimi!" Grant said.

"I'm glad you're safe, but don't do that again!" Mimi said. "You must be hungry!"

"STARVED!" Grant said, "and glad to eat dinner...instead of be dinner!"

That night, Larry was happy to finally get some rest. He snuggled into his sleeping bag and picked up his pillow to fluff it. A piece of paper fell out of the pillow case and onto his lap. In the same scary scribble as the rest of the clues it said:

> Larry me, Larry me, he's laid to rest in the hot prairie, his mark is left for all to see.

Larry grabbed his sister's shoulder and shook her till she woke up. Grant and Christina heard the **commotion** and sat up, too.

"I found another clue," Larry said. He was terrified.

14
WHAT'S UP WITH CHUCK?

After a night of fitful sleep and worry, Grant and Christina were ready to get out of Scotts Bluff. The last clue had been the worst of all. It sounded like something terrible was going to happen. And it called Larry by name! Christina was beginning to look at everyone on the trail as a suspect. The mystery man, or woman, had to be on the wagon train with them; there was no doubt in her mind. She tried to focus her attention on the next stop which Mimi promised would be interesting.

After another long, bumpy, dusty ride, a group of crumbling, gray buildings appeared against the Rocky Mountains rising in the distance. They were surrounded by a series of more modern buildings built in a large circle. In the middle was a courtyard of bright green grass.

"Straight ahead are the ruins at Fort Laramie, Wyoming," Van yelled back to the wagon trail. "We'll spend the rest of the day here."

The kids jumped out of the wagon as soon as Papa stopped it. Larry looked distracted and worried. He was holding the folded clue in his hand. His fist was clenched, crumbling the paper.

"Hey, guys," Grant said, trying to sound encouraging, "Mimi says this place used to be an Army fort built to help protect travelers on the Oregon Trail. They've got guns and stuff to look at. I'll stick with you, Larry, and make sure you're safe."

Larry looked up at Grant with a weak smile.

"Alright, I guess we can try to have fun," he said. "But I might stay close to the Army stuff. I'm not sure how much you can do with those mini-muscles of yours," he added, teasing Grant.

Grant lifted his arm and flexed, frowning at the tiny bump that rose up from his bicep.

"Haven't had much time to work out on the trail," Grant said in a deep voice. Larry laughed.

Larry was ready to get the creepy clue out of his mind and Fort Laramie did look inviting. He gladly followed Grant to the large, white, plantation-style building that was home to the Army Outpost Museum.

Inside, the boys were amazed by all the artifacts.

"Look, Grant!" said Larry. "It says here that Fort Laramie was built to protect pioneers from Indian attacks."

"I wish we could see a real live Indian attack!" Grant said.

"Yeah, as long as we could be on the winning side!" Larry remarked. "I wouldn't want anyone counting coup on me. SCALPS!" he added, when Grant look puzzled.

Larry pointed to a glass case in the corner.

"Those must be their uniforms. They look so thick!" Larry said. He stood in front of a mannequin wearing a gray wool uniform with a patch of the American flag on the right arm. "Could you imagine wearing that in this heat?"

"No way!" Grant said, feeling his face get sweaty just from the thought. "I hope that was their winter outfit!"

"Yeah," said Grant, "but in a big, winter snow, that was probably not near warm enough."

The girls stayed back at the ruins, exploring the old hallways that used to be Fort Laramie. As Christina walked on the smooth stone ground, she felt like an authentic pioneer. Her cotton dress blew ever so slightly in the prairie wind. She looked out over the plain and imagined lines of wagons driving by. She peered down the hall and imagined soldiers peeking out the windows of the fort searching for Indians and waving to the wagon trains. Christina could explore this Wild West town for hours, lost in the history. But Narci looked worried.

"Narci, what's wrong?" asked Christina. "Are you still thinking about the clue?"

"I'm just so worried about Larry," Narci said. "That clue sounded so threatening and I think he might be in trouble."

"Well, Grant's with him," Christina said, trying to sound encouraging.

"I know, but I can't shake this feeling that something bad is going to happen to him," Narci said. "The clue said he is 'laid to rest for all to see'!"

"Maybe the clue doesn't mean something bad will happen," Christina said. "Let's explore. Maybe we can find something here that will help us understand what it means. I have a feeling that when we figure it out, it won't be as bad as we think."

Narci looked skeptical but she was up for anything that would help Larry.

"Let's get down to business," Christina said in her detective tone. "Who are our prime suspects?"

"Well, there's Van and Chuck...and everyone else on the wagon trail," Narci said with a sigh.

"Right. So, let's start with the clue and work backward," Christina suggested.

"OK," Narci said. "Last night we were stuck on the bluff. Then Chuck brought us back to camp. Then Larry found the clue."

"Chuck! He saved us last night. How did he know we were at the bluff?" Christina asked. She mulled the clues over in her mind. "Maybe he hid the clue! Maybe that's how he knew we'd be there!"

"But I thought you said it couldn't be Chuck," Narci said, confused.

"The first rule in a mystery is, never rule out anything!" Christina said. "Come on!"

Christina grabbed Narci's arm and both girls ran out through the ruins. Christina stood in the grass courtyard and scanned the buildings surrounding the fort looking for any sign of Chuck. In the distance she thought she saw a man with a long, curly beard slip through the door of the Artillery and Wagon Museum.

"I think he's over there!" Christina cried.

Narci and Christina ran to the museum and opened the bulky wooden door. Inside were displays of old wooden wagons a lot like the ones in their train. In the corner, a life-size group of pioneers sat around a campfire. "Narci!" Christina whispered anxiously. "Is it just me, or does that guy by the fire look just like Chuck?"

Narci looked where Christina was pointing. "I don't see him," Narci said.

Christina looked back, afraid she might see Chuck staring right at her. The man leaning over the fire was gone!

"That had to be Chuck," Christina said. She suddenly felt terrified. Was Chuck following them? She glanced around the museum. They were the only ones in the building. "Let's get out of here!" Christina said, pulling Narci toward the door.

"Wait!" Narci said suddenly. "Look, over there!"

The door at the back of the museum was cracked slightly. "I think he might have gone out that door!" Narci said.

The girls cautiously ran toward the door. They slowly pushed it open and looked at each other in fear. The door creaked and heat poured into the museum. Outside, the girls could barely see in the bright sunlight. When their eyes adjusted, they saw the dusty prairie...and their parked wagon train!

"Do you think Chuck went back to his wagon?" Narci asked.

"I guess we should go check it out," Christina said.

The girls slowly crept around the side of the parked wagons, trying not to be seen.

"Which one is his?" Narci asked. *CLANG!* The sound came from two wagons back. Narci looked at Christina and they both tiptoed toward the wagon.

When they were only steps away, Christina heard a loud commotion that sounded like banging pots and pans. They could see Chuck's big, muddy boots standing at the back end of his wagon.

"You don't think he's got Larry, do you?" Narci whispered.

"No," Christina said confidently. "Come on. We're going to get to the bottom of this."

Christina bravely stepped around the wagon and stood face to face with Chuck. He seemed taller than she remembered. He looked down at her and frowned through his scraggly beard.

"What are you doing out here?" he asked. His voice seemed to boom across the prairie.

"Um, we were hungry so we thought we'd get a snack from the wagon," Christina said. She hadn't planned to lie, but Chuck looked like he needed a good reason.

"You stay there," he said. He climbed up into his wagon and disappeared. Christina felt like running but she had to see if Larry was safe. She waited, her knees wobbling.

Narci stared at her from the front of the wagon with a terrified look.

Christina jumped when Chuck reappeared again. In his hand was a metal bowl.

"I made this for lunch," he said, gruffly. "Take it."

Chuck dropped a bowl of hot chili into Christina's hands. She looked down in disbelief. Chili? It was almost nice of him.

"Uh, thanks," Christina said. Then she ran as fast as she could back to the fort. Narci followed right behind her.

15
LARRY ME, BURY ME

The girls were out of breath when they got back to the ruins. They collapsed on the hard floor and tried to catch their breath.

"What happened to you?" Grant asked. He and Larry walked toward the girls. They wore blue and orange feathers around their heads and had black paint smudged under their eyes like Indian warriors.

"I think the better question is what happened to you?" Christina said.

"We were at the Army Outpost Museum and they were giving free face paintings," Larry answered. "We got a little carried away."

Narci giggled for the first time all day. She was glad to see her brother happy.

"Where have you two been?" Grant asked.

"It's a long story," said Narci.

"Well?" Larry asked, expectantly.

"We thought we'd figure out the clue," Christina explained. "So we followed Chuck and found him in this exhibit, and then he was gone, and then we followed him outside, and then we were at our wagon train, and then we saw Chuck, and he went into his wagon, and then he gave me THIS!" Christina held out her bowl of chili. Most of it had sloshed out during her frantic run.

"Oooh, chili!" Grant said. "Can I try it?"

"Go for it," Christina said. She handed the bowl to Grant, who hurriedly shoveled the spicy mixture into his mouth.

"Why did you go after Chuck all by yourself?" Larry asked, ignoring Grant's loud smacking.

"I was worried," Narci said, embarrassed. "I thought something was going to happen to you."

Larry smiled at his sister. "Thanks, Narci," he said. "But you shouldn't have gone off by yourself. Plus, you knew I'd be safe with Grant to protect me."

"Huh?" Grant said. He looked up, his lips covered with red chili remains.

"Nothing," Larry said, with a smile.

"Kids!" Mimi yelled across the fort. She and Papa walked toward them with a pamphlet of Fort Laramie in their hands. "We want you to see something."

The four kids met Mimi and Papa and followed them out of the fort and down a trail. At the end of the trail was a small round stone with a name carved on it.

"This is a sad story," Mimi said. "But I wanted us to remember his bravery."

She read in her pamphlet about a boy named Joel Hembree: "He was six years old when his family started on the Oregon Trail. In a terrible accident, he was crushed under the wheels of his wagon. His grave is the oldest known grave on the Oregon Trail."

"Wow," Christina said, "That's so sad."

"He was so young," said Narci.

"I think we'll leave you four here to have a moment with Joel," Mimi said. She grabbed

Papa by the arm and they walked back up the trail.

"Remember how big our wagon wheel was?" Grant said. "No wonder he was crushed."

"'He's laid to rest in the hot prairie, his mark is left for all to see,'" Christina repeated from the clue. "I think the clue was talking about Joel, not Larry!"

"But why did it call Larry by name?" Narci asked, not convinced.

"Larry me, Larry me," Grant repeated, trying to figure out the clue. "Larry me. Oh, Larry me! I get it, guys. 'Larry me' sounds like Laramie. The clue was leading us to Fort Laramie!"

"I think you're right!" said Larry.

Narci jumped in excitement and hugged her brother. Christina and Grant gave each other a high five. Another solved clue and they were still safe. But as they walked back to the wagon train, Christina couldn't help but wonder how the mysterious clue got under Larry's pillow. Who was leading them on this wild goose chase?!

16
WRITING ROCK

The next stop on the trail was the place Narci had been looking forward to seeing since the wagons pulled out from Independence, Missouri. When she saw the large rock mound in the distance, she almost couldn't hold in her excitement.

"There's Independence Rock!" Narci shouted.

The enormous rock stretched across the prairie like a sleeping giant. It wasn't tall and steep like Scotts Bluff, but it was just as impressive. Their whole wagon train wasn't as long as one side of the rock. In fact, the wagons looked tiny next to the huge natural wonder.

Narci said. "This is one of the most important landmarks on the Oregon Trail."

"Why? Grant asked, "it's just a rock."

"Not *just* a rock," Narci said. "If you look closely, the rock is covered with hundreds of names of the pioneers that passed by on the Oregon Trail."

"Wow!" Christina said, intrigued by the history.

When the wagon train pulled next to Independence Rock, the kids stood in awe. Crowds of tourists snapped pictures of the names carved in the stone.

"This is it!" said Narci. "Let's go."

Grant, Christina, and Larry followed Narci to an area of the rock that wasn't crowded with tourists.

"I've been looking forward to this for days!" Narci said. "I want to find the signature of my grandmother!"

"You mean your great-great-great-great, adopted grandmother!" Christina and Grant said in unison.

"Yes," Narci replied. "Help me look for 'Narcissa Whitman'."

The four kids scanned the rock, trying not to miss any names.

"I can't make out most of them," Christina said. "They're all smudged and faded."

"There's one I can read," Grant said, pointing to a carving:

DV HERBERT
JULY 8, 1897

"July eighth!" Narci said excitedly.

"What's so great about July eighth?" Grant asked.

"Independence Rock was an exciting stopping point for the pioneers," Narci explained. "They left in the spring, like we did. By the time they made it to Independence Rock it was usually around July fourth."

"Cool!" Christina said. "What a great way to celebrate Independence Day!"

The kids spent the rest of the afternoon walking slowly around the rock and reading the inscriptions. They were carved into the rock, written with chalk, or painted on with tar. When the sun moved low in the sky, Larry looked up.

"Guys, we better get back to the wagon," he said. "We don't want another 'bluff incident'."

Narci sighed. She hadn't found any sign of Narcissa's signature.

"Can I take one last look around?" Narci asked.

"Just hurry," Larry said. "We need to get back before dark."

Narci scanned the rock one last time. This time something shiny and black caught her eye. She walked toward it, hoping to see her grandmother's name. Instead, she found a sentence written in the same handwriting as the clues. It was painted on with tar that was still dripping and hot.

"Guys!" Narci called.

"What is it?" Larry said. The kids ran to her side.

"I think I found another clue!" Narci pointed up toward the dripping tar sentence.

Grant, Christina, and Larry stared in disbelief. They read,

Oregon may be close, but the journey is still long. Don't believe all you see, Independence doesn't make you free.

"I didn't see this here a minute ago," Christina said. "Where did it come from? Someone must have done this recently."

"Independence doesn't make you free?" Grant said, confused. "That doesn't make sense."

"Yes it does," Narci said quietly. "I think it means that just because people signed Independence Rock doesn't mean that they made it all the way down the Oregon Trail. Lots of people turned back when they realized Oregon City was still months away. Some had wagon accidents, encountered Indian attacks, or got sick with cholera. Even died."

"How do you know all this?" Christina asked.

"I did a lot of research on Independence Rock," Narci said. "I wanted to know as much as I could about it. I felt sure I would find Narcissa's name here."

"But why do you think someone would leave that clue for us?" Grant asked, confused.

"I don't know," Larry said. "I'm just glad it didn't say anything about danger, graves, or curses!"

The kids trudged back to camp as the sunset turned the sky three shades of purple. Tonight they could relax. Another mysterious clue was solved! And this time, they didn't even have to figure it out!

As the sun set behind Independence Rock, a long shadow appeared in the distance. Near the rock, a figure hunched over, carrying a bucket of dripping black tar!

17

A JOLLY GOOD STAY AWAY!

The next day, the wagon train bumped along the trail in a field next to an interstate highway. Cars, trucks, and tractor trailers flew by at what seemed like lightning speed. Grant and Christina spent most of the day walking next to the wagons and waving at the passing cars.

"Look!" Christina said, pointing toward the highway. "There's the sign for the Idaho state line!"

"That means we're only one state away from Oregon," Grant said. "Woooo-Hooo!"

Just then, the wagon train made a sharp turn, veering away from the highway.

"Where are we going?" Grant asked.

"I don't know," Christina said. "But I see something ahead."

The wagons headed for a tall, white, square wall.

"Foooort Hall!" Van yelled back.

"He always does that right on time," Grant said, scratching his head. "He really is a wagon master extraordinaire!"

The wagons pulled to a stop in front of the towering white wall. Its rough, stucco-like texture and bright, white color contrasted with the chocolate-brown wood on the huge wooden door.

Everyone on the wagon train gathered in a circle in front of the door.

"This here's Fort Hall," Van said to the group. "Well, actually, it's a replica of what Fort Hall probably looked like in the 1800s. It was occupied by the British until the United States claimed the Oregon Territory in 1846. British soldiers who lived in this fort tried to discourage pioneers from going any farther. Some people listened, some didn't. But anyhow, this is our last official stop before we get to Oregon City."

Grant look at Christina with a big smile.

"But don't get too excited yet," Van went on. "We'll celebrate when we make it to Oregon City. We'll only spend about an hour here. If we want to make it to Oregon in time, we have to hit the trail hard. So enjoy the fort, because we've got a long couple of days ahead of us."

Grant, Christina, Narci, and Larry looked at each other with dread.

"We've had a couple of long days ahead of us this whole trip!" Grant said.

"Let's look around," Christina said, ignoring her brother's complaint. "We've only got a little bit of time here."

Van opened the massive wooden door and the kids followed the rest of the crowd inside. In the middle of the fort was a spacious grassy area with benches.

"I've got an idea," Larry remarked, looking at a staircase on the inside of the fort wall. "Let's climb to the top of the fort and see what we can see."

"OK!" Grant said.

The four kids climbed up the stairs to a narrow walkway on top of the fort wall.

"Look, over there," Christina said, pointing to a little hut on the corner of the wall roof. "Let's go see what's inside."

The kids tiptoed down the narrow path. They held on to the sides of the wall to keep their balance. One trip and it was a long way down!

Inside the tower was a sizeable, square room with little windows. The kids sat on the white, stucco floor and peered out at the impressive view.

"Look," Larry said, "they've still got a British flag flying in the fort." A red, white, and blue flag flapped in the prairie wind, attached to a pole on the top of the fort wall.

"Would you like a cup 'o' tea?" Larry said in a silly British accent, holding the flag in his right hand.

"I'll have tea with crumpets, sir!" Grant replied, in an even worse British accent.

"What's that?" Narci asked, pointing to a small blue ribbon hanging from the corner of the flag. Larry grabbed it and held it steady against the wind.

"You won't believe it," Larry said. "Another clue!"

"Up here?" Christina asked in disbelief. "Who would know we would come up here?"

"I don't know but let's hear it," Grant said. He didn't seem one bit surprised at finding another clue. "Like I said, a good mystery has a way of never letting you forget!"

Larry read the clue slowly.

> Beware, the raging river flowing there cannot be crossed but with much care, only venture if you dare.

"It sounds a lot like the warnings Van was talking about," Christina said.

"Narci, you got anything?" Grant was hoping for another instant answer.

"Sorry, not this time," Narci said. "I guess it's warning us that the river ahead is dangerous."

"Van did say it'd be a rough couple of days," Larry said.

"But he didn't mention anything about a river," Christina said.

"Well, I don't know about you," Grant chimed in. "But I'm getting pretty tired of these foreboding clues. I just want to know why someone would try to ruin our trip! So far, every danger the clues have warned us about haven't even been real. All it's done is made us worry."

"Grant has a point," Larry said. "Maybe we should just forget about the clue and try to enjoy our last few days on the trail."

"I think that's a good idea," agreed Narci.

"Christina?" said Grant.

"Yeah, forget it, OK," Christina said, her voice trailing off.

Christina followed her friends down the wall and back to the wagon. She said she would forget the clue, but she couldn't ignore the looming mystery at hand.

18
ACHIN' FOR SOME BACON

The *bump, bump, bump* of the wagon had a different tune the next day. Grant couldn't help but feel a little sad that the trail was almost through. It's not every vacation that you get to drive a horse-drawn wagon and eat bacon three meals a day!

The kids quickly learned that Van wasn't kidding when he said the next few days would be hard. The wagons kept rolling until the sun went down, and they were off on the trail before the sun came up the next morning. Around lunchtime the wagon train crossed the Oregon state line.

"Oregon City, here we come!" Grant yelled.

There was a buzz of excitement in the air. Narci was drawing every last picture she could fit in her sketch book. Larry and Grant were busy dreaming up cowboy and Indian adventures in the Wild West. Everyone seemed excited about crossing into Oregon except for Christina.

"Hey," Grant said, "why the long face? We crossed into Oregon, you know."

"Yeah, I know," Christina said sadly, "not even the prairie dogs underground could miss your announcement!"

"Of course!" Grant said. "So, are you excited? We're in Oregon. This is the *Oregon* Trail. That's got to be good, right?"

"I guess I'm just not ready for this trip to end," Christina said.

"I know, I don't think Mom's going to let us eat this much bacon at home," Grant lamented.

"No, not that," Christina said, annoyed. "I mean, the trail's almost over and we haven't figured out the mystery."

"You're still thinking about those dumb clues?" Grant said.

"They might not be important to you," Christina said. "But I just can't figure it out. There's got to be more to this mystery. I just know it."

"I say the mystery's history!" Grant said. He nudged his sister with his elbow trying to get a smile out of her. "Well, if you don't mind, I've got a pretty important battle with an Indian named Munching Grass to get back to."

Christina couldn't help but giggle a little.

"Ha! Got you!" Grant said.

Christina's giggle did not last. She was going to figure this mystery out, one way or another.

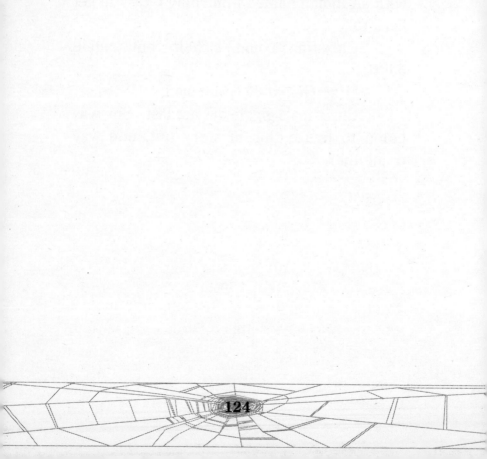

19

DA, DA, DA, DALLES!

"Turns out Oregon's a pretty big state," said Grant. He couldn't hide his disappointment. Hours had passed since they crossed the Oregon state line and still there was nothing but prairie.

The sky ahead loomed gloomy and dark. Grant heard thunder in the distance. He felt like the trail was never going to end.

"Hey guys!" Christina said. Her voice sounded surprisingly happy. She'd barely spoken ten words since morning. "A river!"

Grant, Larry, and Narci stuck their heads out of the canvas top. Sure enough, a wide, lazy river stretched across the land in front of them.

The wagon train was heading straight for the water! To make matters worse, the thunder and lightning were getting louder and louder, closer and closer. Grant didn't understand why his sister sounded so excited.

"A river, just like the clue said," Christina explained, almost giddy. "I'll bet there's another clue ahead!"

Narci looked at Christina like she was crazy. "I'm not getting out of this wagon and searching for a clue in a thunderstorm!" she said.

"Well, you three don't have to help," Christina said confidently. "I can do it on my own. I'm going to figure out this mystery."

At the edge of the river, the wagon train came to a stop. Van's wagon was first in line followed by theirs.

Van stepped down from his wagon. "Looks like we're in for a double-doozy," he said. "The Dalles River is our last major obstacle. After this, it's smooth sailing. And hopefully you'll be sailing on land, not down the river! Anyhow, we're going to drive the wagons one by one across the river. I'll go first to show you how it's done and help anyone along the way who needs it. Chuck'll be the last one across—he knows what to do. But since it seems that there's a storm a brewin', we best get started as fast as we can."

Van took his horses' reins and gave them a loud SNAP! The horses took off into the water, leaping with every step. "GIDDY UP! C'MON GIRL! YAH!" The horses slowly trudged through the river, struggling against the rising water.

The kids watched anxiously. Just as Van's wagon seemed to dip too low into the water, he shouted one last "GIDDY UP, GIRLS!" The horses struggled up the opposite shore. Van was safe and sound.

"Whew!" Grant said, "I almost thought he wouldn't make it."

Van looked back at the wagon train. "The key is to keep the horses going!" he yelled across the water.

"Do you think you can handle it, Papa?" Christina asked her grandfather, who looked a bit concerned.

"You just hold on, Christina, we'll make it," Papa said. He sounded more confident than he looked.

"Let's go!" Van shouted, motioning for Papa to come across.

Papa slapped the reins and yelled, "YEE HAW! Ooops, I mean GIDDY UP!"

The horses lurched forward. The kids held on tight in the back of the wagon. They watched the water rise up the wheels and the side of the cart.

"Whoooaaaah!" Grant yelled in a shaky voice. The water was so high it was trickling in the back of their wagon. Just when Grant was about to let out a full-fledged scream, the horses jolted the wagon up the shoreline and out of the water.

Everyone in the wagon let out a sign of relief. Papa's sigh was the biggest of all.

They waited safely on shore for the rest of the wagons to cross. Each crossing was a nail-biting experience, but all the wagons made it safely to the shore. Now it was time for the chuck wagon.

Christina noticed that for a split second, Chuck looked anxious. He kept glancing at the sky that was gradually getting darker.

Just as Chuck was about to slap the reins of his horses, a CRACK of thunder blasted through the air. The noise spooked Chuck's horses and they jolted his wagon into the river.

"WHOAH!" Chuck yelled, trying to get control of the reins.

"Is he OK?" Grant asked, looking up at Van.

"Chuck's done this a million times," Van said, trying to look confident. "He'll get control."

CRACK! FLASH! Chuck's horses bucked and kicked in the river. Chuck's wagon swayed in the water.

"We've got to help him," Christina said.

"It's too deep," Narci said, "If we go out there, we might get hurt."

Christina ignored Narci's advice and ran toward the edge of the river.

"Christina, what are you doing?" Papa yelled after her. She didn't answer.

Grant and Larry followed her into the water. Narci watched for a minute, hesitating, and then ran after the other three.

"Chuck, don't worry," Larry called out. "We're going to help you out!"

Chuck looked up. When he saw the kids, panic spread across his face. "Go back! Go back!" he yelled.

The kids waded over to his wagon. Larry grabbed the horses' harnesses.

"Larry, be careful!" Van yelled from the shoreline.

Larry tugged on the harnesses while Narci tried to calm the horses with soothing words.

"It's not working!" Grant yelled. "We've got to figure out another way."

Larry let go of the reins and waded back near Chuck's wagon.

"Chuck, what can we do?" Larry yelled up to him.

"Nothing!" Chuck said. "You kids shouldn't be out here. Are you crazy? Go back to shore!"

Just then a clap of thunder rattled the ground. This time, the horses reacted by running up and out of the river. Chuck's wagon tossed and turned up the side of the bank. CRASH! CLANK! Pots and pans flew everywhere. Pieces of white paper fluttered through the air. Christina noticed a book fly out and land on the muddy shore.

When the chuck wagon made it up the shore line, Chuck pulled the horses to an abrupt stop. He slowly stepped down from the wagon.

"Chuck, are you alright, buddy?" Van asked, running toward him.

"Yeah, just a little shaken up," he said, running his hands down his tousled beard. "Where are the kids, are they alright?"

Chuck and Van were met with four angry faces. Christina held a history textbook covered in mud. Grant, Narci, and Larry clutched handfuls of wet, white paper.

"It *was* you all along," Christina shouted. "You planted the clues; you tried to ruin our trip!"

"Yeah and there's more clues here," said Grant, holding up a handful of notes scribbled in Chuck's messy handwriting. "You weren't going to stop!"

"How could you?" Narci said. "We worried the whole trip. I thought my brother was in danger!"

"Wait, kids, I can explain," Chuck said. He slowly walked to the kids with his hands out. "This is a misunderstanding."

"What was going to be your final clue?" Larry yelled back at Chuck. "What kind of dangerous thing were you planning next?

"Kids!" Mimi shouted, surprised by how upset her grandchildren seemed. "Let Chuck explain."

"Mimi??" Christina said in disbelief. "You're in on this too?"

"So are your Papa and me," Van admitted, stepping closer to the kids.

"What?" Grant asked, totally confused.

"I hid the clues because I wanted you guys to have fun on the trail," Chuck said.

"Fun? With those clues?" Christina answered.

"I saw you four kids the first day of the trail at Independence." Chuck said. "I thought if I hid some clues, it would make the trip more interesting. I wanted you to experience the trail as the first pioneers did. I never meant any danger. The clues were to help you understand the danger the pioneers went through. I kept a close eye on all four of you. I got good at predicting where you might go so I could hide the clues where you'd find them."

"But why?" Grant asked. "You don't even like kids."

"I do like kids!" Chuck said. "I used to be a teacher."

Christina's eyes widened in shock.

"I wanted my students to be excited about learning," Chuck continued. "But most of them just didn't seem to care. I gave up on teaching. So, I came out here where my buddy Van was a wagon master. He let me ride along with him as long as I cooked the meals."

"So let me get this straight," Grant said. "You gave us a mystery to solve to *teach* us something."

"I'm truly sorry," Chuck said. "I like you kids. I didn't mean to cause harm."

"We knew what Chuck was doing," Papa added. "We wouldn't have let anything bad happen to you."

"I knew there was *more* to this mystery!" Christina said, half excited, half shocked.

"Come on guys," Mimi said. "Let's get you in some dry clothes. Oregon City is just over that hill."

20

WE'RE OFF TO SEE THE CITY, THE WONDERFUL CITY OF...OREGON!

Oregon City was just about the prettiest town Christina had ever seen. The rolling hills, bold flowers, and lush, evergreen trees were in stark contrast to flat plains. She felt pretty again in jeans and a pink stretch top. All was back to normal.

The wagon train had pulled into Oregon City the night before. The adventure and mystery were over. Larry and Narci's parents were waiting for them at the end of the trail with an adorable furry puppy. Christina hugged Narci, and Grant shook Larry's hand. They promised they'd write and talk often—or at least send text messages!

Now, Christina, Grant, Mimi, and Papa toured the End of the Oregon Trail Interpretive Center. It was a museum filled with stories of the more than 2,000 pioneers who crossed the Oregon Trail.

"They should slap my picture up on one of these exhibits," Grant joked. "I went through a lot too, you know!"

"I guess this'll be our last goodbye," Van's voice was loud and deep in the museum. He walked toward Grant and Christina with another man. "It sure has been a pleasure leading a wagon trail with you two." Van took off his cowboy hat and gave Grant and Christina a bow.

"And I hope you still like the Oregon Trail after everything that happened," said the man standing next to Van.

"I'm sorry," Grant said to the man. "Do I know you?"

"It's me, Chuck!" the man said. "I know, I look different."

Chuck was wearing a sports jacket and tie with khaki pants. His beard was shaved off and his hair was cut and styled nicely. He wore a pair of brown glasses.

"I'll say!" Christina said in amazement.

"You can call me Professor Charles," Chuck said. "You kids inspired me to start teaching again! I haven't taught a class in ten years. I start my first day tomorrow. If I have a class full of kids half as good as you two, it's going to be a wonderful year."

Christina looked up at Chuck with a big smile.

"Well I have some news of my own," said Grant shyly. "I'm not going back to school. I am going to stay out here and get a job on the wagon trail. Not in the chuck wagon...but something. OK, Mimi? Papa?"

"NO!" said Mimi and Papa together.

"We understand how you feel," said Papa, "I could sure stay, too."

Christina giggled as Mimi gave Papa her evil eye. "But your parents will say you have to finish school first," Papa added.

"Besides," said Chuck. "I don't think..." He put his closed fist over Grant's hand and opened it. Out popped a toy rattler!

Grant squealed, jumped away, and dropped it. "You're not quite ready, yet, son!" Professor Charles said.

Grant frowned and rubbed his hands on his pants. "Well, maybe not," he grumbled. "But I will be...NEXT YEAR!"

Well, that was fun!

Wow, glad we solved that mystery!

Where shall we go next?

EVERYWHERE!

The End

The Oregon Trail, Part II
by Christina

Well, if you don't think America is big and wide, just try crossing it in a covered wagon. Now having done so, I just really can't imagine how those pioneers did it! Of course, many did not live to get to their new homes in the West. We got tired of the eternal rolling along those rough ruts, the dust, heat, cold, and same old food. But they had encounters with Native American Indians not happy to see newcomers. Some got diseases and died. Wagon train accidents were common. River crossings were dangerous. And, there was no "911." You gotta have a lot of respect for the early pioneers. They were brave. Me? I'm tired and dusty and ready for a HAMBURGER!

Now...go to
www.carolemarshmysteries.com
and...

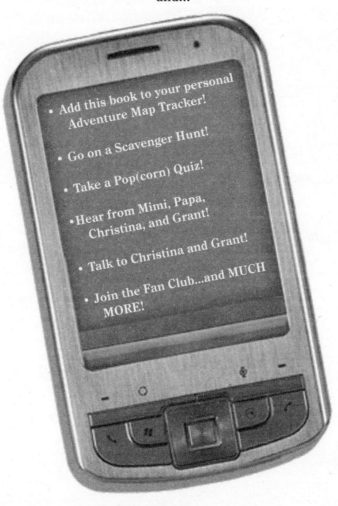

- Add this book to your personal Adventure Map Tracker!

- Go on a Scavenger Hunt!

- Take a Pop(corn) Quiz!

- Hear from Mimi, Papa, Christina, and Grant!

- Talk to Christina and Grant!

- Join the Fan Club...and MUCH MORE!

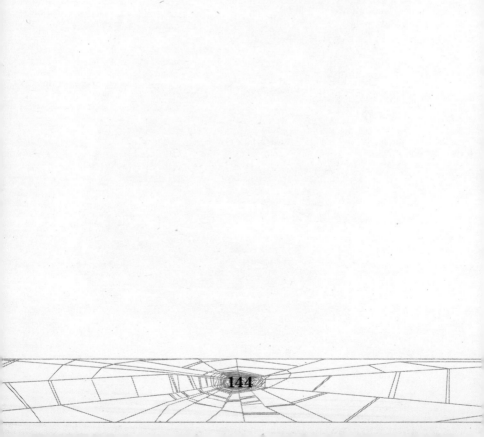

GLOSSARY

bison: big, wooly, horned mammals that live on the prairie

canvas: strong cloth used to cover the wagons on a wagon train

cholera: deadly disease usually caused by drinking contaminated water

chuckwagon: the wagon used to store food and cooking supplies

coup: act of bravery against an enemy

hardtack: hard, unsalted biscuits eaten on the trail

prairie schooner: nickname for a covered wagon

wagon master: the person in charge of leading the wagons along the trail

SAT GLOSSARY

outpost: a fort that is far away from a settlement or other forts

confident: to feel good about yourself

commotion: a loud disturbance or movement

terrify: to frighten

sense: to have a feeling about

Enjoy this exciting excerpt from:

THE MYSTERY AT Mount Vernon

Home of America's First President, George Washington

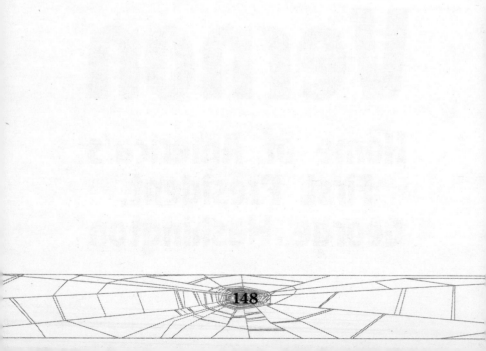

1
CHOP PHOOEY

Christina felt tense for no good reason. It was springtime in Washington. The cherry trees throughout the city, a gift from Japan many years ago, were covered with blooms that reminded her of thousands of tiny, pink butterflies. The sun was shining, and birds were singing like rock stars. Still, something wasn't quite right.

Christina and her brother Grant had been to the nation's capital many times with their grandparents Mimi and Papa. Each time, her dream of visiting Mount Vernon, home of America's first president and Revolutionary War hero, George Washington, had never happened. But this time, Mimi had promised. Papa pushed his cowboy hat back on his head, leaned against a cherry tree, and sighed. "When that woman finds a library, she loses all track of time," he grumbled.

Mimi, a mystery writer, had spent most of the week at the Library of Congress. She was researching a new mystery—one so mysterious she wouldn't even tell them what it was to be about. Christina had a sneaky suspicion it had something to do with the Revolutionary War.

Papa glanced impatiently at his watch. "Sure hope she didn't get lost," he said.

Grant had gone into a nearby toy shop to kill time while Christina and Papa waited for almost an hour outside a bike rental shop near Washington. It wasn't their usual way of getting around, but what better way to get to Mount Vernon and at the same time enjoy the area's most beautiful season?

Christina had just noticed black clouds on the distant horizon when a sudden whirlwind scooped cherry blossoms off the sidewalk and sent them in a pink blizzard straight toward her. Blinded, she froze as something grabbed at her shoulders.

Christina blinked hard but saw nothing but a fuzzy, gray blur passing her face. Was a rascally raccoon playing pranks on her? Another hard blink revealed a glint of silver from a hatchet blade. Raccoons don't carry hatchets, Christina thought in panic. Is there a madman on the loose?

"Papa!" Christina screamed, stumbling to the spot where she had last seen her grandfather.

Papa caught Christina just as she tripped. "Whoa there, little darlin," he said in his deep, charming cowboy voice. "You know I love to dance with ya, but is the sidewalk the best place?"

"Someone's after me," Christina stammered and grabbed Papa around the waist. "And he's got a hatchet."

Christina felt Papa's belly jiggling with laughter.

"I think you better look again," he said between good-natured guffaws.

Christina rubbed her eyes. The fuzzy, gray image came into focus. It was only Grant!

"Looks like your brother has found some nifty souvenirs," Papa said with another laugh.

Grant struck a pose with the hatchet. What Christina had thought was a raccoon was a gray wig like old men wore in the 1700s.

"Guess who?" Grant said.

"A little old lady having a bad hair day?" Christina suggested.

Grant frowned. "If you knew anything about history, you'd know I'm George Washington," he said.

"You may think you're George," Christina replied. "But I cannot tell a lie. You've got that wig on backwards. The ponytail is supposed to be in the back, not coming out of your forehead."

Grant eyed the blossoms that had landed on Christina's shoulders. "Well, you should really do something about your bad case of pink dandruff," he said.

"Ha, ha, ha," Christina replied, rolling her eyes and brushing the blossoms from her shoulders.

"Here goes!" Grant shouted, raising the

hatchet into position to give the nearest cherry tree a chop.

"Grant!" Mimi yelled. "Stop!" She scurried toward them, her red high heels wobbling on the cobblestone sidewalk. "Don't you dare hit that tree!"

Grant shot her a mischievous grin. "No worries, Mimi," he said. "It's only plastic."

"You need to do some more research on that cherry tree tale," Mimi said. "Most historians believe the famous story of a young George Washington chopping down his father's favorite cherry tree and then telling him the truth never really happened."

"You're kidding!" Grant said with a disappointed look.

"That's right," Mimi confirmed. "A preacher named Mason Weems used that story to teach boys like you not to lie."

"Guess that means I can never tell Christina how beautiful she is again," Grant said with another mischievous grin.

"If we don't mosey down that trail,"

Papa said, "those black clouds are going to rain on our parade."

Mimi changed from her red heels into her red tennis shoes. Of course, Papa had also rented a bike in her favorite color. As they buckled their helmets, the bike shop owner stepped outside to see them off. An old man with cloudy blue eyes, he gave them a warning that Christina thought was as ominous as the clouds.

"I'd be careful if I were you," he said. "There have been some strange things happening at that old mansion."

2
WAYWARD WIG

"Beat you to the top!" Grant hollered. He wheeled his lime green bike past Christina and pedaled hard. The gray ponytail of his wig wiggled furiously under his helmet.

"Don't forget, it's not called Mount Vernon for nothing!" Christina yelled after him. While waiting for Mimi, Christina had studied the trail map. She knew this final climb would be the worst, so she paced herself. She wasn't planning to let Grant win. She knew the best way to beat him would be to let his blast of speed wear him out long before he reached the top.

Christina waved to Mimi and Papa, lagging like Sunday drivers far behind, and stood up on the pedals of her blue bike. The springtime air was unusually humid and heavy for April, and it made Christina's shoulder-length, brown hair bushier than Grant's wig. At least I'm not likely to run into any of my friends, she thought.

Grant had almost reached the crest of the hill when he stopped and planted his feet on the pavement. Christina smiled with satisfaction. She knew her brother would run out of steam before he won the race.

"What's the matter?" Christina crowed as she flew past. "Run out of gas?"

Grant didn't reply. Christina pumped the pedals and gasped when she reached the crest. Standing stately beyond a sea of freshly mown grass was perhaps the United States' most historic home—Mount Vernon. The simple, white mansion with its red roof practically glowed in front of the dark clouds that still threatened their visit.

"Can you believe that George Washington actually slept here?" Christina asked her brother. He gave no answer. "Grant?"

Her brother had plenty of time to catch

up by now. Christina looked in her bike mirror. She could see Grant's bike on the trail edge, but he was nowhere to be seen!

Christina knew Grant could never pass up an opportunity to use the bathroom outdoors. He had probably slipped behind a bush to do just that. But the bike shop owner's warning still swirled in her head. Christina turned around and aimed her bike back down the hill. "Grant!" she called. "Where are you?"

Naked branches just sprouting green buds clawed at Christina's clothes while she pushed through the brush beside the trail. "You better not be hiding!" Christina warned. She braced herself, waiting for Grant to jump out and say, "Boo!" Nothing happened.

"You can't scare me, I know you're here somewhere!" Christina yelled. She took more careful steps but stopped with a squeal. Something furry was tickling her toe. "OOOOOH!" she yelped, expecting to see a wild animal about to bite her foot. What she saw frightened her even more. It was Grant's gray wig.